Jelly Bean Jumble

Candy Fairies

Jelly Bean Jumble

HELEN PERELMAN

ILLUSTRATED BY
ERICA-JANE WATERS

ALADDIN
NEW YORK   LONDON   TORONTO   SYDNEY   NEW DELHI

ALADDIN

An imprint of Simon & Schuster Children's Publishing Division

1230 Avenue of the Americas, New York, NY 10020

First Aladdin hardcover edition February 2013

Text copyright © 2013 by Helen Perelman

Illustrations copyright © 2013 by Erica-Jane Waters

Also available in an Aladdin paperback edition.

For information about special discounts for bulk purchases, please contact Simon & Schuster Special Sales at 1-866-506-1949 or business@simonandschuster.com.

The Simon & Schuster Speakers Bureau can bring authors to your live event. For more information or to book an event contact the Simon & Schuster Speakers Bureau at 1-866-248-3049 or visit our website at www.simonspeakers.com.

Designed by Karina Granda

The text of this book was set in Berthold Baskerville Book.

Manufactured in the United States of America 0113 FFG

2   4   6   8   10   9   7   5   3   1

Library of Congress Control Number 2012941020

ISBN 978-1-4424-6000-3 (hc)

ISBN 978-1-4424-5297-8 (pbk)

ISBN 978-1-4424-5298-5 (eBook)

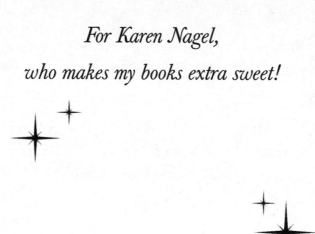

For Karen Nagel,
who makes my books extra sweet!

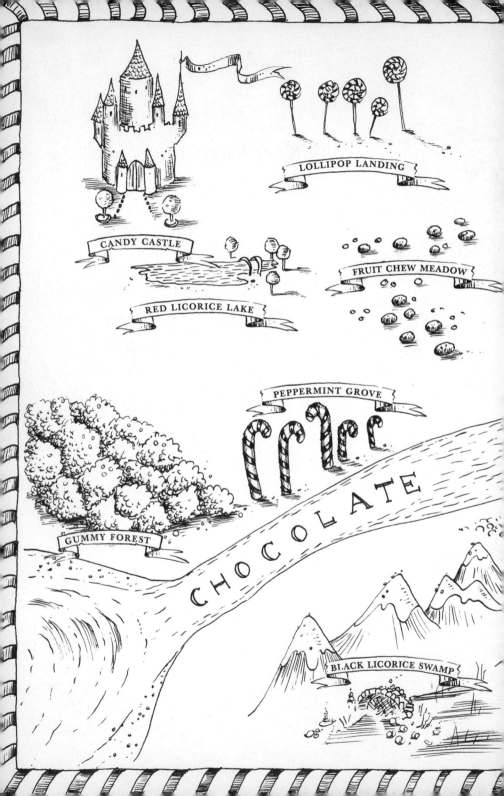

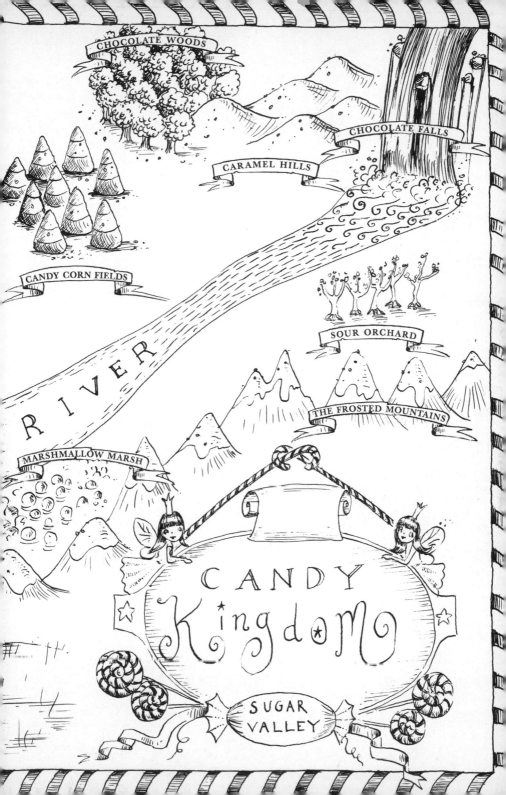

Contents

CHAPTER 1

Sweet Surprise Lunch

The sun shone down on the Royal Gardens at Candy Castle. Berry the Fruit Fairy sat under a lollipop tree with her friend Raina, a Gummy Fairy. "It feels like everyone in Candy Kingdom is outside today," Berry said.

"On a day like this, it's hard to stay inside,"

Raina replied. She tilted her face up toward the sun's rays.

Berry smiled. It was the first warm day of spring, and all the fairies in Sugar Valley were buzzing around. After the chilly winter, the warm sunshine was a welcome feeling.

"Thanks for meeting me for lunch today," Berry told her. "I'm sorry I missed Sun Dip last night."

Sun Dip was a time when Candy Fairies gathered to talk about their day. During the last moments of daylight, Candy Fairies shared stories and sweet treats. Yesterday Berry had missed out on seeing her group of friends.

"Did you finish planting the jelly bean seedlings?" Raina asked.

Berry's wings fluttered. "Yes," she said. "I

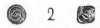

needed the extra time last night. The seedlings are getting so tall. I planted them all."

"Princess Lolli is going to love the new crop of jelly beans," Raina said, smiling. "Our basket is going to be *sugar-tastic*!"

Berry and her friends were making a special basket for Princess Lolli's upcoming journey to see her sister, Princess Sprinkle. Princess Sprinkle lived on Cupcake Lake and ruled over Cake Kingdom to the north. Each sister brought the other the best of her kingdom's crops to share when she visited.

On her last visit, Princess Sprinkle had brought beautiful cupcakes, cakes, cookies, and brownies. The Cake Fairies were known for their tasty treats. The Candy Fairies always had a feast during those visits. For Princess Lolli's trip, Berry had wanted to give the fairies in Cake

Kingdom a special sweet treat of her own.

"Cocoa and Melli showed us the basket last night," Raina said. "They worked very hard and it is beautiful."

"And did Dash find the nighttime mints?" Berry asked. "I know she was worried about getting the right size mint for Princess Lolli to see near the Forest of Lost Flavors."

Raina shivered. "Oh, I don't like thinking of that place," she said. "All those white, flavorless trees . . ." Her voice trailed off.

Berry had heard many stories about the creepy forest from Raina. The Gummy Fairy loved books and owned the largest collection in Sugar Valley. There was plenty written about the Forest of Lost Flavors. The wide forest divided the land between Candy Kingdom and

Cake Kingdom. Most Candy Fairies stayed far away from the eerie forest. Nothing grew there anymore—no candy crops at all. Now there were just tall white trees without any flavor. That forest was not somewhere a fairy would want to be without any light, and it was scariest at night.

"I am sure Princess Lolli is going to love our basket," Berry said. "It is an honor to make her one for her trip. I don't remember the last time she went to see her sister."

"Princess Sprinkle has come here for the last few visits," Raina remarked. "Princess Lolli must be excited." She looked over at Candy Castle. "I wonder if she gets nervous about traveling such a far distance. I would!"

Berry reached for her fruit nectar drink. "I saw Butterscotch yesterday. She was looking forward

to the flight. If I could ride Butterscotch there, I
wouldn't be afraid."

Butterscotch was a royal
unicorn. She was a beautiful
caramel color with a deep-
pink mane. She often took
Princess Lolli on long voyages.

"Maybe," Raina said thought-
fully. "I'm not sure that's a trip
I would want to make with
Butterscotch, or any unicorn."

"I would take a unicorn ride any day!" Dash
said, landing next to Berry.

"Dash!" Berry exclaimed. "Lickin' lollipops,
you scared the sugar out of me."

Dash giggled. "Sorry," the small Mint Fairy
said. "When Raina told me she was meeting

you for lunch, I had to join in the fun."

"And so did we!" Melli said, flying in with Cocoa.

Berry looked at the Caramel and Chocolate Fairies in front of her. "You came to see me?"

"Sure as sugar!" Cocoa said. "We missed you last night."

"Were you talking about Princess Lolli's trip?" Melli asked. She sat down next to Berry. "I know Berry wishes she could go. Besides Meringue Island, Cake Kingdom is the leading place for fashion, right, Berry?"

Berry shrugged. "Well, Cake Kingdom does have some sweet styles," she said, thinking. "But I've never been there. I've only read about it in *Sugar Beat* magazine."

The five fairy friends settled down to eat their

lunch. It wasn't often that they got to see one another during the day. Usually, each of the fairies worked in a different part of the kingdom on her own candies. This was a sweet surprise lunch.

They had just finished eating when a burst of chilly air lifted Melli up off the ground. "Brrrr," she said, shivering. "What is going on? It was such a beautiful morning!"

"I think there's a storm coming," Cocoa said. She looked up to the sky and saw the dark clouds rushing overhead. "Bittersweet, I was so hoping for another warm night."

"That isn't going to happen," Dash said, slipping on her vest. She carefully wiggled her silver wings through the slots in the back. "Nothing like a brisk spring evening to get the mint flowing," she added. "And I have got some mighty mints

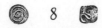
8

to tend to. See you fairies later!" In a flash, Dash was gone. She wasn't known as the fastest fairy in Sugar Valley for nothing!

Melli wrapped her shawl tighter around her waist. "What about your seedlings, Berry?" she asked. "They are not going to like this blast of cold."

"Oh, it's not so bad," Berry told her. She looked up at the sky. "Winter has passed. Sure as sugar, the sun will warm us all tomorrow with another sunny day. I can't wait!"

Berry's friends shared a worried look. But they all agreed that by Sun Dip the next day they'd put their candies and finishing touches on the basket. They knew Princess Lolli was counting on them. And none of them wanted to disappoint the sweet fairy princess.

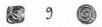

CHAPTER 2

Sour Face

During the night a bitter storm traveled through Sugar Valley. The strong winds blew cold blasts, leaving a layer of frost all over the northern part of Candy Kingdom. Berry slept soundly through the night, not hearing the storm at all. Her work in Fruit Chew Meadow over the last few days had made her very tired.

When the Fruit Fairy woke up, she looked out her window. *What happened?* she thought. At first she thought she was still dreaming. She rubbed her eyes. But there, on the fruit slices outside her window, was frost! Thick frost. Cocoa had been right about a storm coming. And what a storm it had been!

"Oh no! The jelly bean plants!" Berry exclaimed. Her heart was racing as she looked out on the white, frosted gardens. She had to get to Fruit Chew Meadow! She wasn't sure what she would find when she arrived.

As Berry flew over the meadow, her heart was pounding. She had been so proud of those plants! She had tried new flavors and had carefully selected the seeds to create bold, bright oranges, reds, yellows, purples, and even pinks for this new crop. She had hoped these beans would be some of her finest work. But Berry's eyes widened when she saw her plants. Heavy ice weighed down the large leaves. Her once-tall seedlings were hunched over. The bright colors of her new spring candy were buried beneath the ice.

"Oh, sour sticks," Berry sighed. She leaned over

for a closer look. As she carefully brushed the ice off the leaves, her fingers tingled from the cold.

"Are you the fairy who planted those?" a voice behind her called.

Berry turned to see Razz, a know-it-all Fruit Fairy. She had the same name as Berry's grandmother, but was not nearly as sweet. Razz was standing right behind Berry with a mean look on her face. Her blond hair was in a high ponytail clasped with a lemon sparkle clip. "Those poor seedlings," Razz muttered. She crossed her arms tightly across her chest. "Planted by a Fruit Fairy who didn't know any better."

Razz had no business saying such bitter words. She was a little older than Berry and often tried to tell her what to do. She might have been a Fruit Fairy, but she always had on a sour-candy face.

 13

"If these are your plants," Razz went on, "you should tend to them right away." She flapped her large orange wings. "A fairy with more experience would have known to wait until *after* the first spring frost to plant."

"The weather was perfect for planting," Berry burst out. She glared at Razz. Any other Fruit Fairy would have offered to help instead of pointing out the problem. Razz's bitter attitude was making everything worse.

Razz shook her head. "Aren't you friends with Raina? Isn't she that Gummy Fairy always quoting the Fairy Code Book?" Her blue eyes shot an icy stare, and Berry shivered. Then Razz chuckled. *"I read in the Fairy Code Book . . . ,"* she taunted, trying to sound like Raina.

Berry took a deep breath. It was true that

Raina always had the Fairy Code Book with her and was quick to quote from it. But there was such helpful information in the fairy history book. Berry didn't like the way Razz was talking about one of her best friends. Hot feelings were bubbling up inside of her, and she wanted to lash back.

"They'll be fine," Berry snapped. She glared back at Razz. She wasn't about to let Razz make her feel worse.

"Well, good luck with *that*," Razz said, tossing her ponytail. And then she flew off.

Alone in the meadow, Berry thought about what to do next. She was still bubbling inside. Razz just made her so red-cherry mad! Maybe she had jumped a little too quickly to plant the seedlings, but she had so desperately wanted

Princess Lolli to take a fresh, new crop with her to Cake Kingdom.

"Not this time," she said with a heavy sigh. Her jelly beans didn't look as if they stood a chance.

Berry sat down on the cold, frozen ground. This was not her first crop of jelly beans. She had planted plenty before. She should have known better. Berry gripped her hands into fists. "Oh," she muttered. "I should have said that to Razz! This is not my first crop of jelly beans!"

For a long time Berry sat looking at the plants. She wondered what would happen to the crop. She looked up at the blue sky. The storm had passed, but would there be another? Or would the sun come out and warm up the meadow? She knew that cold weather at this stage of

growing jelly beans could change their flavor. There was nothing Berry liked less than a tasteless jelly bean. She slumped down and put her head in her hands.

Then Berry realized something. "Sweet strawberries!" she exclaimed. "Maybe Razz did say something helpful."

If there was any fairy who might know what to do, it was Raina. With that huge library of hers, maybe there'd be some information about how to tend to frozen seedlings. For a moment Berry's wings dipped down low to the ground. She didn't want to be entered in the Fairy Code Book as the Fruit Fairy who had ruined the first spring jelly bean crop.

But maybe there was still time to save them. In a flash, Berry headed to Gummy Forest.

Bitter Cold

Berry shivered as a cold gust pushed her wings back. She fought against the wind and headed down to Gummy Forest. Thinking back to yesterday, she remembered how proud and happy she had been. The warm sunshine had made the ground perfect for planting, and she had finished her work in the Fruit Chew

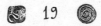

Meadow. Now her tasty, prize-winning jelly beans were freezing. If only she could turn back time and hold off on planting.

The wind made her wings feel heavy, but Berry traveled on. She had to get to Gummy Forest and talk to Raina.

As she arrived Berry noticed the land wasn't as frosted as in Fruit Chew Meadow. Maybe the tall trees in the forest protected the gummy plants. In Fruit Chew Meadow there were no trees, and the field was more open.

Raina fed the gummy fish at Gummy Lake every morning. Berry checked there first and felt a wave of relief when she saw Raina standing on the shoreline.

"Raina!" Berry called out. She flew over to her friend. "I am so happy you're here!"

Raina nearly dropped her basket of flavor flakes. When she saw Berry, she rushed over to her. "Berry, did you hear that storm last night?" she asked. "The winds were whipping around here. Many of the animals are still in hiding."

Berry shook her head. "I slept through the whole storm," she admitted. "This morning was a surprise. When I woke up, I saw there was an icy frost all over the meadow. And on the jelly bean seedlings!"

"Oh, sweet sugar," Raina replied, shaking her head. "I was afraid you were going to tell me that. This is more than a spring frost." She looked worried.

"I was hoping we could do some research," Berry said. "Maybe there is a story in the Fairy Code Book about a spring storm that could help us figure out how to save the frozen crops."

"Maybe," Raina said. "Tell me, how are the seedlings? How are the leaves?"

"They are very weak," Berry told her. Her fingers still tingled from brushing the ice off the jelly bean leaves. "I removed all the ice this morning. But I am afraid the damage has

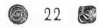

been done. If I don't help them now . . ." Berry stopped talking. She couldn't finish her sentence. She looked into Raina's kind eyes. She knew her friend understood how hard it was for her to talk about the damaged crops.

"Why don't you head back to my house," Raina said. She threw more of the flavor flakes in the lake. "While I finish up the gummy feedings, you can start doing some research."

"Thanks, Raina," Berry said, flying off. Raina had the best library in all of Candy Kingdom. If there was a book that could help her, she would find it in Raina's library. "I'll see you soon."

Inside Raina's house Berry was overwhelmed by the selection of books. She started pulling down books from the shelves. Flipping through the pages, she searched for anything about a

spring frost. She flew from one end of the room to the other. Not one book she looked at helped her at all.

"What happened in here?" Raina exclaimed. She stood at the door with her mouth gaping open.

Berry looked up from the book in her hand. She saw the mess she had made of Raina's home. There were open books tossed around the room. Berry could tell from Raina's expression that she was not happy. Raina was all about order and kept her books neatly organized and lined up on her shelves.

"Sorry," Berry said softly. She gently closed the book she was holding and put it carefully back on a shelf.

Before Raina could say anything, a sugar fly appeared with a message. Raina took the note from the sugar fly and read it out loud. "Princess Lolli has canceled her trip!" Raina exclaimed. She looked over at Berry. "The storm must have caused more damage in the kingdom than we thought if she is not going to Cake Kingdom."

"We should send messages to our friends to meet up now," Berry said. She wrote quick notes and handed the letters to the sugar fly. "Please take these to Dash, Melli, and Cocoa," she said. "Thank you!"

Berry watched the sugar fly soar out into the gray sky. A few of the ice patches on the ground were beginning to melt. But now that Princess Lolli had postponed her trip, Berry had to wonder what the rest of Sugar Valley looked like.

"It's a bitterly cold happening . . . ," Berry muttered as she flopped down in a chair. She

glanced around at all the books. "One of those books must have the answer," she said.

"Maybe," Raina said. "The trick is to know where to look." She blew her long bangs off her forehead. "What a mess, Berry."

"I'm sorry," Berry mumbled.

The fairies continued to do research as they waited for their friends to arrive. Berry tried not to think about what her seedlings were looking like now. Maybe the morning sun would warm up the ground and keep the seedlings safe. She hoped that her friends would get to Gummy Forest as soon as possible. This was an emergency!

4

The Right Spot

Not long after the sugar fly left Gummy Forest, Berry found herself surrounded by her good friends. Melli, Cocoa, and Dash had come as soon as they had heard the news. Now all five fairies were huddled up in Raina's library.

"Hot caramel," Melli said, shaking her head.

"It looks as if there was a storm in here. Who blew through here?"

"Um, that would be me," Berry confessed. "I'm desperate to find information about a spring frost." She flew up to a high shelf. "We can clean up later."

Dash picked up a pile of books from the center table. "Maybe we can search faster if we put away the books that you looked through already."

Raina gave Dash a sweet smile of thanks. "We should have a system here," she said.

"We don't have time for a system," Berry snapped. "Everyone start looking!"

Cocoa looked from Berry to Raina. She shuddered when she caught the icy stare they shared. "And I thought the patches of frozen chocolate

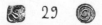

in Chocolate Woods were bad," she mumbled.

"You know how Raina likes to keep her library," Melli whispered.

Berry saw that Raina was upset, but she couldn't stop her search now.

"This is not typical of a spring storm in Sugar Valley," Berry declared. "There have been storms to start the spring, but none like this." She flew to a shelf across the room for another book. "Maybe this book will help shed some light." She took *Shades of Spring* in her hands and flipped through the thick book.

"I can't believe you haven't found any information," Dash said. "There are so many books here! None of them mentions a spring frost?"

Berry closed *Shades of Spring*. "I'm trying," she said. She didn't want to be grumpy, but she had been researching all morning. "Sweet strawberries, you'd think we would have found some helpful bit of information already." She glanced at the books lying in heaps around the room.

"What about the other damaged crops?" Dash asked. She popped a mint into her mouth.

"All those young seedlings and early buds are going to be ruined."

Berry felt all eyes staring at her. She wanted to be strong and show her friends that she was in control. But the weight of the day was pushing her down. Since the frost was still in Sugar Valley, Berry knew that meant the ground was still rock-hard sugar soil. There was no way her seedlings were going to grow or last.

"How are the other parts of the kingdom?" Raina asked, looking around at her friends. "I haven't been out of Gummy Forest today."

Cocoa spoke first. "I think the storm hit hardest to the north, so Candy Castle and Fruit Chew Meadow were covered in thick frost. Areas farther east weren't so bad."

Berry gasped. "Has anyone heard from

Princess Lolli?" She had not even thought about the castle and what could have gone wrong there. "Maybe we should fly up to the castle and see what is going on there. I hope she is all right. Let's go!"

Berry led the way to the castle. She was sad to see the lollipop tree where they had been sitting yesterday covered in a white dusting of ice. The Royal Gardens looked sleepy and cold, buried under a thick coat of ice.

Raina reached out and gave Berry's arm a squeeze. "Let's go inside and see Princess Lolli," she said.

The palace fairies were all busy trying to spread heaters around the garden. There were no palace guards to announce their arrival. One of Princess Lolli's advisers, Tula, was standing

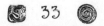

33

near the front gate. Berry grabbed Raina's hand, and together they flew over to her.

"Tula," Berry said, slightly out of breath. "How is Princess Lolli?"

Tula pushed her jewel-coated glasses up on her nose. "Oh, it's a bitter day," she said. "The storm took the northern part of the kingdom by surprise."

"Is Princess Lolli . . . Is she okay?" Raina asked.

Tula regarded the two fairies standing in front of her. "Yes, she is fine," she said. "Her heart is just heavy from the weight of the storm." She unrolled a scroll in her hands. "Here is the growing list of the areas hit by the cold blast."

"How can we help?" Berry asked, jumping in.

"We're trying to figure out the damage first,"

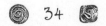

Tula said, smiling at the fairies. "We will let you know."

Berry's wings drooped to the floor. "And Princess Lolli is not going to Cake Kingdom at all?"

Tula rolled her scroll up again tightly. "It doesn't look as if she will make that journey," she said. "So many Fruit Fairies have fruit chews and lollipops that are in danger of being ruined. The princess didn't feel it was right to leave the kingdom."

"Princess Lolli must be very disappointed," Berry said to Tula. "She was looking forward to that trip."

"Yes, I was, but I can't leave the Candy Fairies now," Princess Lolli said, coming up behind Berry.

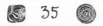

"Berry, how are your jelly beans? How is the rest of Fruit Chew Meadow? The report this morning was not good."

Berry gasped. She hadn't thought that she'd get to see the fairy princess. She rushed over and gave her a hug. It seemed like the only thing she could do. Plus, she wanted to hide her face. She was embarrassed that Princess Lolli knew about her frozen jelly beans.

"Fairies, come closer. I know if we all work together, we'll be able to get through this difficult time," the princess said bravely.

Tula stepped forward. "Princess Lolli, you have an emergency meeting with Tangerine and JuJu. They are quite upset about the damage to their lollipops. You have to leave immediately."

"Yes, yes," Princess Lolli said, rushing off.

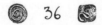

"Oh, I hope this blows over quickly," Tula said as they all watched Princess Lolli fly off. Tula then tucked her scroll in the satchel on her shoulder. She turned to Berry. "It's too bad," she said, full of sorrow. "Princess Sprinkle knows a lot about these storms. There have been many like this in her kingdom. I was hoping she could help. But communication has been difficult since the storm, and she is too far away to do anything for Candy Kingdom now."

Berry's ears perked up. What was Tula saying? Was there a story in the Fairy Code Book that she and her friends had missed?

"Raina," Berry whispered to her friend, "we were only looking at the history of Candy Kingdom. But what about Cake Kingdom?" Her eyes sparkled with the hope of finding a solution.

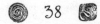

"Maybe we weren't looking in the right place!"

She raced over to her friends. They had to get back to Raina's and do more reading. Perhaps the answer was not in Candy Kingdom's history, but in a different kingdom's history.

CHAPTER 5

Sprinkle of Hope

As the five fairies made their way back to Gummy Forest, Berry flew up next to Raina.

"There must be a book that has stories just about Cake Kingdom, right?" Berry asked.

"Yes, of course," Raina said. "And I know just the book." When she got home, she went right to her library and then let out a heavy sigh. "Well,

I *used* to know exactly where to find the book."

Berry felt bad for Raina. Usually, Raina was able to think of a title and know exactly where the book was located. But not in this mess.

"Can I help you?" Berry asked.

"I think that you helped enough," Raina mumbled. "The book is called *Cake Kingdom: A Recipe for the Ages*," she called out. "If anyone sees it, give a holler."

Dash ducked underneath the table and brought up a strawberry-and-vanilla-colored book. "Found it!" she cried.

"What a pretty book," Melli said.

"Pretty delicious," Dash added.

Raina put the large volume on the table, and the fairy friends gathered around.

"Why didn't I think of this before?" Raina asked. She lifted the heavy cover of the book and gently turned the thin, creamy pages. "Cake Kingdom is way up north, and sure as sugar they have had spring storms like this. There are four Cake Kingdom books that go together. One of them might have the answer." Raina flipped open to the contents page. "This one doesn't talk about storms. We need the other books. . . ." Her voice trailed off. "If we can find them."

"Cocoa and I will look for the matching books," Melli offered.

"Me too!" Dash called.

Berry watched her friends scatter and search for the missing books. "I am sorry that I made such a mess," she said to Raina. She looked down at her sparkly shoes. "I am messing up everything."

"You aren't messing up *everything*," Raina told her. She smiled at her friend. "Just my library!"

"Princess Sprinkle is so wise," Cocoa said as she looked for the pink-and-white books. "I loved hearing her talk about chocolate brownies last time she was here. I hope there is an entry about one of their storms and what the Cake Fairies did to help save their sweets."

Dash rubbed her stomach. "Just thinking about Cake Kingdom is making me hungry," she said. She licked her lips. "Remember those cupcakes that Princess Sprinkle brought last time?"

"Oh, I do," Cocoa said. "Those were *choc-o-rific!*"

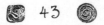

"And they were so beautiful," Melli added. "Remember all those clever candy toppings? She was so sweet to share with all the Candy Fairies."

"Come on," Berry pleaded. "We need to focus." She leaned closer to a book. Seeing Princess Lolli so sad had spun Berry into more of a frenzy. Now more than ever she wanted to feel as if she were helping out.

The fairies looked through and read the many history books on Cake Kingdom. Sadly, none had stories of such an early frost with any clever and warm solutions.

"I'm getting cold reading about all these frosts," Melli said. "I say we break for a snack."

"I second that!" Dash shouted. She pulled out a sack of mint treats from her bag. As she did a copy of the *Daily Scoop* fell out.

"I haven't read this week's newspaper," Cocoa said, reaching for the copy. "I heard the Sugar Pops have a new song coming out."

Berry rolled her eyes and continued reading through the thick book in front of her. She couldn't be bothered with the Sugar Pops right now.

"Wait a second," Raina said, moving closer to Cocoa. She pointed to a page in the newspaper. "Look! There was a storm at Cupcake Lake early this week," she read over Cocoa's shoulder.

Cocoa read out loud, "'There was a burst of cold that left an unexpected ice frosting over the crops.'" She looked around at all her friends. "'The soil was frozen, and the winds knocked down several stalks and trees.'"

Berry squeezed her hands together. "Remember, Tula was talking about a very recent storm!" She

flew over to sit next to Cocoa. "Keep reading, Cocoa," she begged. "Maybe the article tells about a solution for frozen crops."

"Huh," Cocoa said, turning the page.

"What?" Berry said, leaning closer. "Why did you stop reading?"

"There is no answer written here. The article just ends." Cocoa scratched her head, puzzled.

Berry reached over and grabbed the paper. "How can that be?" she gasped.

"Maybe the problem was solved after the article was written," Melli offered.

Sometimes, Melli's sweet-as-caramel attitude bothered Berry, but right now, she didn't mind.

"Or maybe there is no solution," Berry said bitterly. She walked away from the table and

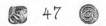

over to the front window. She didn't want to see her friends' faces.

"Berry, we'll find a way to save the jelly beans," Dash said. "We always come up with a plan. We need a little more time."

"But we don't have time," Berry snapped. As soon as she said those words, she felt bad about her tone. She didn't mean to hurt Dash's feelings. She turned to her minty friend. "I'm sorry," she said. "I shouldn't be so harsh."

"I think we're all feeling the pressure," Melli stated.

"I just wish Princess Sprinkle were *here*," Raina said. "I bet she knows how to help the frozen crops."

Berry snapped her fingers. "Jumping jelly beans!" she exclaimed. "That's the answer! We

need to bring Princess Sprinkle here to Candy Kingdom."

Melli raised her eyebrows. "That sounds like a *sugar-tastic* idea," she said. "But . . . how are we going to get Princess Sprinkle here?"

"In order to get her *here,*" Cocoa said, "we need to get *there.*"

"And *there* is very far!" Dash added.

Raina stood up. "Berry, Cocoa is right. We'd have to pass through the Forest of Lost Flavors. That is not a quick trip."

Berry understood the problem. But she was not going to let that ruin her plan. "If Princess Lolli was going to fly Butterscotch there, why can't we fly a unicorn there?"

"But we don't have a unicorn," Dash replied, breaking thc silence.

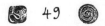

Melli shot Dash a look. "Don't be so minty," she scolded.

"It's a good point," Berry said, smiling at Dash. "I will take care of the ride," she said reassuringly. She winked at Raina. "You map out the trip."

"Berry . . . ," Raina began.

Berry held up her hand. "I will meet you back here at Sun Dip," she said, calling over her shoulder as she flew off. "This is going to be a sweet plan. You'll see!"

Berry raced to Fruit Chew Meadow to find her ride. For the first time since she had seen the frost on the leaves outside her window, she had a sprinkle of hope.

CHAPTER
6

A Magic Ride

When Berry arrived at Fruit Chew Meadow, she saw that a layer of ice was still spread over the ground. The afternoon sun hadn't warmed up Sugar Valley enough to get rid of the ice. The sight made Berry sigh heavily. The longer the ice stayed around, the more her

jelly beans were at risk of losing their flavor.

Berry tried not to let her sadness stop her. As she flew over the meadow she noticed that other Fruit Fairies had pushed the ice off the leaves of the fruit-chew plants. Berry shivered as she looked over the many different crops.

By the northern corner Berry spotted what she was looking for and flew fast. There was

beautiful Lyra, the white unicorn who guarded the fruit-chew plants.

Lyra was a small unicorn, and her sweet voice was said to be one of the secrets that made the fruit chews in the meadow so delicious. Not long ago, Mogu, the sour old troll, had tracked salt into the meadow. The salt from Black Licorice Swamp had been caked on the troll's shoes, and he had brought the salt dangerously close to Lyra. Salt was like poison to the unicorn, and she had gotten very sick.

Berry didn't like to think about that time. She was still angry at Mogu for pulling that salty stunt. But Berry and her friends had helped Lyra. She was sure that Lyra would help her and her friends now.

"Hi, Lyra," Berry called out. She patted the

unicorn and slipped her a sugar cube. Lyra's colorful mane blew wildly in the wind.

Berry noticed that Lyra looked concerned. Her extra-long eyelashes shaded her large eyes, but Berry could tell what she was thinking. This cold snap could damage her crop as well.

"The fruit chews are still covered in frost," Berry said, bending over to examine the plants. "They are the heartiest of the fruit candy, so they should be fine." She saw that the fruit chews were still colorful and the leaves were dry. "I can't say the same for my jelly beans." She shuffled her feet. "I planted a little early this year, and I am scared that I've ruined the entire crop."

Berry felt that she could be honest with Lyra. She was especially close to the unicorn. Maybe it was because they both tended to the fruit-chew

candies, or just because they shared a love of fruity sweets. If Lyra said no, Berry and her friends would be in a sour state. Berry had to pose the question to Lyra in the right way. Now more than ever the fairies of Candy Kingdom needed Princess Sprinkle.

Lyra tilted her head and looked at Berry. Sensing that there was something on the Fruit Fairy's mind, she motioned for Berry to sit down near the fence.

Berry's eyes brimmed with tears as she followed Lyra. When she sat down on the chilly ground, Berry blurted out her request. "My friends and I want to go to Cake Kingdom and bring Princess Sprinkle back here."

Lyra nodded. She understood what Berry was about to ask. Berry felt that the unicorn

had even been expecting the question.

Berry looked down at her hands. "But we can't make the trip on our own. We need help. As you know, Cake Kingdom is far from here— past the Forest of Lost Flavors."

Lyra stretched her legs out beneath her.

Berry looked up at Lyra. "Would you take us?"

The white unicorn lifted her head up to the sky. Her pink-and-purple mane blew around her in a burst of color. In the stillness of the moment, Berry held her breath.

"I know it is a lot to ask of you," Berry said. "The trip for a unicorn your size could take two days." She closed her eyes and wished with all her heart that Lyra would agree to the task.

Lyra nudged Berry with her long nose. She was nodding.

Berry leaped up and hugged the unicorn tightly around her neck. "Oh, thank you, Lyra," she sang. "Raina and the others are mapping out the journey now. I know it's a big favor to ask, but I really think Princess Sprinkle will have the answer and will help Candy Kingdom."

Lyra looked toward Candy Castle and then back at Berry.

"No, we didn't talk to Princess Lolli about the trip," Berry told her. "We know she has so much else on her mind. We don't want to worry her." She smiled. "If we can get to Princess Sprinkle and show her what has happened to the crops, she can tell us what to do. Then we can tell Princess Lolli and help save the frozen candy."

The unicorn stood up and shook her body.

"Thank you, Lyra," Berry said again. "I am

going to tell the others. We'll see you tomorrow morning? We can leave from Red Licorice Lake." She gave the unicorn a hug good-bye.

Berry headed back to Gummy Forest to tell her friends the plan. She felt sure that Princess Sprinkle was the key ingredient to making this messy situation better.

CHAPTER 7

Flavorless

The next morning, Berry looked up at the sky to see the welcome and beautiful sight of a unicorn flying. Lyra's mane formed colorful ribbons across the blue sky.

"Lyra's here," Berry announced. She tucked a vine with a bunch of white jelly beans in her bag. She wanted to show Princess Sprinkle what had happened to the crop. "Is everyone ready?" she asked.

"As ready as I'll ever be," Melli said. She gripped Cocoa's hand. "I hope the trip isn't too scary."

"It might be," Cocoa told her. "But we'll all be together."

"And we'll be helping Princess Lolli and all the crops covered in ice," Raina added. "We *must* go!"

"Plus, it's so mint to ride on a unicorn!" Dash squealed, squinting up at the sky. "I can't wait!"

Raina picked up her basket of travel candy and maps. "I hope we can get to the Forest of Lost Flavors before the end of Sun Dip. It will be good to set up camp before dark."

Berry buttoned up her bag. "I think we'll make it in plenty of time," she said. "I hope these jelly beans will be safe. I want Princess Sprinkle

to see the color . . . or missing color."

Lyra landed, and neighed to the fairies. One by one they hopped onto the unicorn's back and steadied themselves for the journey to Cake Kingdom.

"Everyone hold on!" Berry said, turning around to see the lineup of fairies. When she saw that everyone was holding the licorice reins, she leaned close to Lyra's ear. "We're ready to take off when you are," she said.

In a swift gallop and then a powerful leap, Lyra took flight. Her large pink wings flapped in a slow rhythm.

"This is a smooth ride," Dash said, smiling. "Not superfast, but enjoyable."

"A styling ride, for sure," Cocoa added.

As Lyra flew over Sugar Valley and they left the

familiar surroundings of Candy Kingdom, Berry couldn't help but feel a little nervous. None of her fairy friends had ever been to Cake Kingdom . . . or even seen the Forest of Lost Flavors. She knew all her friends were being very brave.

"Let's sing a song," Melli suggested. "You know Lyra loves to sing."

"Sweet idea, Melli," Berry said. She was happy to think of something besides the freezing jelly beans.

The five fairies began to sing as they sailed along the blue sky, away from Candy Kingdom. The sun moved across the sky as time went by. Berry tossed out a blanket for the fairies to wrap themselves up in. The winds had died down, but it was still chilly. After many songs and a few sweet snacks, Raina reached for Berry's

sugarcoated binoculars. Only Berry would have such high-fashion travel gear!

"Sweet sugars!" Raina gasped. She was pointing straight ahead. "That must be the Forest of Lost Flavors!"

Berry straightened up. Ahead of them were tall white branches sticking up in the distance. She shuddered. Thinking about her jelly beans at home, she grew quiet. If they stayed white from the frost, they could be like this forest: flavorless.

"So mint!" Dash exclaimed as they flew over the forest. "It's creepy cool."

"Just like it said in all my books," Raina agreed.

Lyra dipped down a little lower to the ground so the fairies could see the forest. By now the sun was almost gone from the sky, which was a pale grape color.

"Good thing there is a full moon tonight," Melli said, pointing to the large moon above.

"And that I have some handy, dandy light-up-the-night mints!" Dash called. She cracked open a few mint candies as Lyra swooped above the forest.

"Does anyone live here?" Cocoa asked.

Raina put the binoculars back to her eyes. "The book said some trolls live here, but no one has ever seen them. Mogu was spotted here a few times. He has a soft spot for Cupcake Lake."

"Let's hope we don't see any trolls," Melli whispered.

Just beyond the forest was Cookie Crumble Beach, where the fairies had planned to spend the night. Lyra glided down to the rocky beach, and the fairies set up camp. Raina and Melli pitched the tents while Cocoa, Dash, and Berry prepared dinner.

"You must be tired from the flight," Berry said to Lyra. "Let me mix you up a warm, sweet dinner."

The fairies and Lyra finished up their meal. The long shadows from the Forest of Lost Flavors cast an eerie glow, and Melli huddled close to Cocoa. "This place is creepy," she said, looking around. She hugged her shawl around her waist. "I feel as if there are trolls around here," she said, her eyes wide.

"There might be," Raina said honestly. "But I think we're safe for the night."

Berry started to hum a lullaby she had once heard Lyra sing. Lyra joined in. Her soothing voice put everyone at ease and lulled the fairies to sleep. When Lyra stopped singing and lay

her head down for the night, only Berry was awake. She kept thinking about how worried Princess Lolli had looked, and about the other Fruit Fairies. She peeked out of her tent and saw the white forest. Her heart sank as she thought of her own white candy.

Will Fruit Chew Meadow soon be like the Forest of Lost Flavors? she wondered. She couldn't bear the thought. What if Princess Sprinkle couldn't help them, and this was a big flop of a trip?

Berry slipped outside the tent. She flew up to a branch in a tall tree and looked out at Cupcake Lake in the distance. She hoped that tomorrow's visit with Princess Sprinkle would be as sweet as icing on a cake.

CHAPTER
8

A Sugar-Hearted Friend

You can't sleep either?" Raina asked. She had joined Berry on a branch in the moonlight. "Are you thinking about tomorrow?"

"Yes," Berry said. She looked out in the distance. The moon above glowed. "I can't wait to talk to Princess Sprinkle. I remember when we met her

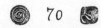

the last time she was in Candy Kingdom. She was so kind and wise."

"Just like Princess Lolli," Raina noted. "I am sure she will help us if she can."

Berry turned to face her friend. "Oh, Raina," she sighed. "What will Fruit Chew Meadow be like with no colorful jelly beans?" She gazed out into the white trees of the forest.

"It took years and years for the Forest of Lost Flavors to become this way," Raina said. She reached out and gave Berry's hand a gentle squeeze. "You should be prepared that Princess Sprinkle may not be able to help us."

"I know," Berry said softly. Her words left a bitter taste in her mouth, and she shuddered. She looked down at her bag lying on the ground with her jelly bean vine. A wave of courage

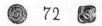

came over her. "Princess Sprinkle will have the answer," she said, trying to be brave. "Sure as sugar, she'll be able to help me."

"Help you or *us*?" Raina asked, raising her eyebrows.

In the stillness of the night, Berry took in a deep breath. Instead of snapping at her friend, she took a moment to let Raina's words sink in. "I've been thinking of my jelly beans, but not of others," she said quietly.

"We all know how you feel about your jelly beans, Berry," Raina said. "But there were other crops affected by the weather. It didn't just happen to you."

"Yes, you're right," Berry admitted. "It feels as if the storm happened to just my crops, but I know that wasn't the only candy damaged by

the storm." She sighed. "I guess I didn't take the time to ask other fairies about their candy." Berry looked down at her sparkling fingernails. "I guess I am just as sour as Razz."

"No," Raina said. "You brought us all here to find a way to fix the jelly bean jumble. And I am sure that whatever we learn from Princess Sprinkle we can use to help other fairies with their crops."

Berry reached out to hug her good friend. "Thank you," she said. "I promise I will help other Fruit Fairies. I don't want anyone to feel as helpless as I do now."

Raina stretched her arms up as she gave a wide yawn. "We should try to get some sleep. Tomorrow is a big day."

Berry drew her breath in sharply. "Don't

move!" she said. She pointed down below to her bag at the bottom of the tree. Two small trolls were sniffing around her bag—her bag with the jelly bean vine!

"Sweet sugar," Raina said with a gasp. She hugged her legs to her chest. "Do you think they saw us?"

"They definitely spotted the jelly beans," Berry said. Her heart was pounding. She had to get those trolls away from her bag!

Quietly, Berry slipped down to the end of the branch. She stuck her hand in her pocket and threw some fruit chews down, away from her bag. As Berry expected, the brightly colored candies amazed the forest trolls. She flew off the branch, sprinkling more candies down on the ground, and the trolls followed the trail away

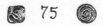

from the tree. Raina flew down and grabbed Berry's bag.

A few minutes later Berry flew back to the tree with a large grin on her face. "I still had some lemon sours in my pocket from a visit with Lemona the Sour Orchard Fairy," she said. "You should have seen those trolls pucker up when they ate one of those!"

"Serves them right for snooping around here," Raina said. She handed Berry her bag. "Maybe you should keep this in your tent tonight."

"Sure as sugar!" Berry told her. "I don't want anything to happen to these. Good night, Raina," she said, flying down to her tent.

"Sweet dreams," Raina replied before they both slipped inside warm shelter for some sleep.

"And thank you, Raina," Berry called to her.

"Not just for tonight, but for everything." She flew over to give her friend a tight squeeze. "And I am sorry that I made a mess of all your books. I promise to clean that all up when we get back."

"I'll hold you to that," Raina said with a grin.

Berry felt lucky to have such a solid, sugar-hearted friend like Raina. It can be hard to point out the truth to a friend, and she was thankful that Raina had done that for her.

The next morning Berry was the first fairy up, the calls of the batter birds the first sounds she heard. Soon their loud cooing woke up all the fairies. Usually, Berry did not enjoy sleeping out. She loved all the comforts of home—including her large wardrobe and all her sparkly accessorics. But she had to admit that the early

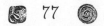

morning sunrise above Cupcake Lake was stunning. The colors were so bright and created a beautiful pattern in the sky.

As she packed up her tent she thought about the trolls last night. While the fairies ate breakfast, Melli, Cocoa, and Dash heard all about the troublesome trolls.

"You tricked them," Dash said proudly.

"Well done," Cocoa told her.

Berry patted her bag. "The jelly beans are safe," she said. "Now let's see what Princess Sprinkle says about them."

Lyra sang out for the fairies to gather around her. Once again they climbed on her back, and Lyra continued the flight toward Frosted Castle. The rising sun glistened on Cupcake Lake and Frosted Castle, which jutted out from behind a

wide hill. Berry noticed that the land below them looked different from Candy Kingdom. There were not as many colors dotting the landscape, and there were more hills. The castle itself was bigger than Candy Castle. It looked older and had many more rooms and towers.

"Holy peppermint!" Dash exclaimed. Her blue eyes were wide as she took in the sight below. "This is an amazing place." She rubbed her stomach. "I am getting hungry just looking around."

"I was wondering when you were going to say that," Cocoa joked. "All that frosting does look quite *choc-o-licious*!"

"With extra sprinkles," Melli added. "Just look at all those colors on the castle. This place is amazing."

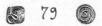

"First stop, Frosted Castle," Berry said.

Lyra flew into the castle courtyard. The tall silver gates were covered with a glittering powdered sugar on top of a thick pink frosting. The five fairies climbed off the unicorn's back and looked up at the castle gates and the tall towers.

"Sweet sugar," Melli whispered.

"This place is much bigger than Candy Castle," Cocoa said, taking in the sight.

"It's much older, too," Raina stated. "This area is the oldest part of Sugar Valley."

Berry reached for the handle on the gate. "Come on," she said.

Behind the gate was a tall fairy. "Welcome to Frosted Castle," he said. He wore a round cap that looked like a cupcake and had a large welcoming smile on his face.

"I am Berry, and these are my friends," Berry said boldly. "We have traveled from Candy Kingdom, and we've come to see Princess Sprinkle."

"Welcome to Cake Kingdom," the guard replied. "I believe the princess is in the throne room." He blew a long, thin whistle, and another guard appeared. "Please take these Candy Fairies to the throne room. They are here to see Princess Sprinkle."

"Are you nervous?" Melli whispered to Berry. "I am!"

"I was more nervous about the trolls," Berry said. She reached up to fix the sugarcoated clips in her hair. "I am just hoping that Princess Sprinkle will be as sweet as her sister."

The guard flew ahead and pushed open a

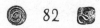

door at the end of a wide hallway. "There are five Candy Fairies here to see you, Princess Sprinkle," the guard announced. He opened the door a little more and then turned back to the fairies. "She will see you now," he said.

Berry led her friends into the room. She took a deep breath. She wasn't sure what to expect from the fairy princess of Cake Kingdom.

CHAPTER 9

The Hot Spot

Princess Sprinkle was sitting on a large throne. Unlike Princess Lolli's throne, it was built up in layers and looked like a cake, with steps to reach the cushioned seat. Berry thought it looked like the drawings of wedding cakes she had seen in some of Raina's picture books. Along the top of the chair were rows of fancy sugar flowers that

Berry couldn't take her eyes off of. . . . How did those Cake Fairies get the frosted flowers so colorful and perfect?

"Hello," greeted Princess Sprinkle. Her face was similar to Princess Lolli's. The sisters looked alike except that Princess Sprinkle had long, straight brown hair instead of wavy strawberry-blond hair like her sister.

The Candy Fairies bowed their heads and said hello. Berry once again took the first step forward. "We are here because there has been a terrible storm in Sugar Valley," she told the princess.

Princess Sprinkle nodded. "Yes, I heard," she said sadly. "The news has been reported. Of course my sister was unable to make the trip to visit." She looked at each of the fairies. "How is my sister? Is everything all right? With the storm, it has been difficult to get messages to her."

Berry assured the princess that her sister was fine. "We have come to see you because we heard you recently had a storm and recovered many of your crops." She reached into her bag and pulled out her jelly bean vine. "Here is what the jelly bean crop looks like now," she said.

"Oh my," Princess Sprinkle said. She took the vine and inspected the candy. "This looks familiar. Our spring storm was not kind to our Brownie Bramble either. We had all the fairies in our kingdom working to help."

"We read about it in the *Daily Scoop*," Raina added. "I guess the story is too recent for the Fairy Code Book."

Princess Sprinkle smiled. "This was a very

 87

recent occurrence," she said. "The storm was just a few days ago. We tried something new this time, and we seem to have saved the crops." She stepped down from her throne and motioned for the fairies to move closer to her. "You see Brownie Bramble?" She pointed out a big window to a large area to the north of the castle. "The fields were covered in ice, which freezes out the flavor," she explained.

"Bittersweet," Cocoa mumbled.

"Exactly," Princess Sprinkle said. "We had to act quickly to warm up the brownies. We placed foil on top of the crops to keep the heat in and warm the soil."

"And this foiling worked?" Berry asked, full of hope.

"Deliciously," Princess Sprinkle said. She eyed

the fairies. "Wait, does Lolli know you are here?"

Berry looked down at the ground. "Um, well, we didn't get a chance to . . ." She was searching for the right words.

"We wanted to surprise her," Raina jumped in. She looked over at Berry and winked. "We thought since she couldn't come to you, perhaps we could bring you to her and offer some help."

Princess Sprinkle grinned. "That is super-sweet of you all," she gushed. "I would love to see my sister. I was planning to send some Cake Fairies to help out with the frozen candies. The foil wrapping worked for us. I am sure it will work for the candy crops. I'd be happy to go back with you."

Berry clapped her hands. "I knew you'd be able to help us!" she cheered.

"First, we have work to do," Princess Sprinkle told them. "We had great success when we steamed up the soil. We filled large vats at Hot Cocoa Springs. The steam from the hot cocoa will keep the inside of the foil tent warm and will hopefully warm up all the candy plants in need of help."

Berry's spirits were lifting. She couldn't help herself and rushed over to Princess Sprinkle to give her a hug. The princess gave her a loving squeeze back. "What sweet fairies you are to come all this way and to care so much about your jelly beans."

Berry looked over at Raina. "This is not just about the jelly beans," she said. "This is for many of the fruit-chew crops."

"Let's take one crop at a time," the princess said wisely. "Jelly beans and other fruit candy are

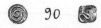

much more delicate than brownies and cookies."

Berry knew the weather played a big part in fruit candy flavoring. She hoped the foil would be the right cure.

Princess Sprinkle took the Candy Fairies to Hot Cocoa Springs. Berry had heard of the hot spot before in magazines and had always wanted to check it out. The springs were a popular destination for fairies to relax and soak in the warmth of the steaming hot cocoa.

"Now, this is *choc-o-rific*!" Cocoa exclaimed as they landed.

The smell of melted chocolate was heavy in the air. There were steaming springs in the ground, all bubbling with hot cocoa.

"What a sweet sight," Berry said. She saw

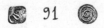

some fancy fairies sitting by the springs, lounging on chairs. They were all wearing very stylish clothes. Berry's mouth hung open. This was a supersweet spot. She had to admit that some of the stress of the day was melting away.

"This is a real treasure in Cake Kingdom," Princess Sprinkle said. "Many fairies come from far and wide to rest here. The springs are one of the most popular attractions here in Cake Kingdom." She looked around. "But the springs are also healing to the crops. Come, let's hurry and fill the barrels with cocoa."

"I wish we could stay here longer," Cocoa whispered to Melli. "I'd love to soak up all this chocolate."

"Maybe we'll come back one day," Melli said, watching Berry's face.

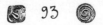

Berry smiled. "Sure as sugar, I want to come back." She glanced over at the large barrels the palace guards were rolling toward the springs. "How will we get these barrels of hot cocoa back to Candy Kingdom?"

Princess Sprinkle blew a whistle and summoned four royal Cake Kingdom unicorns. "This is Red Velvet, Marble, Pound, and Vanilla," she said. The unicorns formed a semicircle and all bowed their heads.

Berry peered up at the glorious unicorns standing before her. Like Butterscotch, they were twice the size of Lyra.

"Their names match their coats," Dash whispered, checking out the unicorns.

"Cake Kingdom unicorns are known to be the

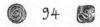

strongest and fastest," Berry stated. She couldn't take her eyes off the handsome foursome. She noticed they were saddled with harnesses for two barrels each.

"Since these unicorns are much bigger than Lyra, they will be able to carry the extra weight," Princess Sprinkle explained.

"We'll have to fly straight to Candy Castle," Raina said. "These barrels will keep the cocoa hot, but not overnight."

"That's true," Princess Sprinkle replied. "You are a smart Candy Fairy, aren't you?"

Raina blushed. "I was just thinking out loud," she said.

"She reads a lot," Dash blurted out.

"Raina is usually right about things," Berry

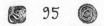

added, smiling at her friend. "We want to get back to Candy Kingdom quickly. All the fruit candy crops need some warmth . . . fast."

The fairies climbed onto the backs of the majestic unicorns. Even Lyra got a ride back to Candy Kingdom on one of the unicorns. The trip back went faster, with Princess Sprinkle leading the way on her golden-cake-colored unicorn. The experienced unicorns knew short-cuts, and they flew a different route home.

As they flew over the Forest of Lost Flavors, Berry took in a sharp breath. She hoped with all her heart that the plan to warm the soil would save the fruit candy crops. The white trees and barren forest made her frightened.

She looked ahead at the lineup of unicorns and the barrels of steaming cocoa. She knew

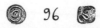

their arrival wouldn't be much of a secret. The sugar flies were going to love this bit of sweet news to spread.

"I hope this works," Berry said to her friends as they flew closer to Fruit Chew Meadow. *It has to work,* she thought.

10

Sweet Endings

When they arrived at Fruit Chew Meadow, the jelly bean plants were still droopy, and all the beans were frozen. Berry knew that the jelly beans were in serious trouble.

"It's like the Forest of Lost Flavors," Dash said. Then her hand flew to her mouth. She didn't mean to sound so bitter.

Berry's eyes filled with tears. She looked to Princess Sprinkle.

"Let's get to work," the princess said bravely.

The fairies gently unrolled the sheets of foil that Princess Sprinkle had packed. They covered the freezing plants and then slipped the barrels of steaming hot cocoa underneath. When they were done with their work, the fields looked shiny in layers of foil.

"I guess we can't drink the cocoa, huh?" Dash asked. Before her friends could answer, she held up her hand. "I know what you are going to say," she laughed. "I'll chew on my mint stick."

Just as they completed the foiling, Princess Lolli appeared. She hugged her sister tightly. "When did you get here?" she asked, grinning. She squeezed her sister's hand. "I'm so happy to see you!"

99

"You must thank the brave Candy Fairies for my arrival here in Candy Kingdom," Princess Sprinkle told her. "They flew to Cake Kingdom and brought me back here."

Princess Lolli turned to the five Candy Fairies. "You flew all the way to Cake Kingdom?"

"Lyra took us," Berry said. "We read about Princess Sprinkle's experience with frost and knew she could help us. I wanted to show her the white jelly beans." She fluttered her wings. "I felt so bad about planting so early . . . and about the other Fruit Chew Meadow crops," she added.

Princess Lolli took Berry's hand. "You couldn't have known about the frost coming," she said. "You and your friends were very clever to go to Cake Kingdom." She smiled at her sister. "I often

don't ask for help when I could use it the most. And you have proved how necessary asking for help can be."

"I'm not sure our hot cocoa plan will work," Berry said. "The jelly beans and the soil are so frozen. . . ." Her voice trailed off. "The jelly beans might be tasteless," she whispered.

"Let's not worry about that now," Princess Lolli said. "We need to wait and see how the soil responds."

The two sisters flew back to the castle to check on the other frozen crops while the fairies set out to cover the other fruit candy crops hit by the storm.

All of a sudden Razz swooped down to Fruit Chew Meadow. "What's going on here?" she asked. She stood with her hands on her hips, a disapproving expression on her face.

 102

Berry stood up and walked over to her. This time she was going to speak her mind. "You'll see," she told her. "We have everything under control."

"Good luck," Razz spat. "Foil over freezing crops?" She threw her head back and laughed.

"Are you sure she isn't a Sour Candy Fairy?" Cocoa whispered to Berry.

At this point, Berry wasn't sure if the jelly beans would get their color and flavor back. . . . All she had now was hope. And she wasn't about to let Razz ruin that feeling.

"We are trying to save the crops," Berry said. "If you want to help spread the foil over the fruit chews and Lollipop Landing, we'd welcome your help."

Razz's mouth fell open. For the first time

Berry saw that the bitter fairy was speechless. She fluttered her wings and quickly took off.

"Wow, Berry," Cocoa said. "You really told her!"

"I was just telling the plain truth," Berry said. "Fairies who don't want to help won't be part of the celebration tomorrow."

"What celebration?" Melli asked.

Berry flew up to the sky and looped around in a graceful circle. "Yes, tomorrow the fruit-chew crops will be saved, and we will have a candy harvesting celebration."

"We can use our basket!" Cocoa exclaimed. She smiled at Melli. "We worked so hard making it, and now we can fill it with yummy jelly beans."

The next morning, when the foil was lifted from the ground, Berry kept her eyes shut tight. She didn't want to look. When she didn't hear any sounds from her friends, she opened one eye. For sure, if the jelly beans were perfect, she would have heard squealing.

"Lickin' lollipops!" she cried. All the jelly beans were white!

"Wait," Raina advised. "I think that before you panic, you should taste one. Remember that sometimes things aren't what they seem like on the outside."

Berry moved slowly over to a jelly bean vine. She carefully plucked a tiny white bean and popped it into her mouth. A burst of orange filled her mouth. "I taste orange!" she cried out. She reached farther down the row and plucked another. This time she tasted a wonderful juicy grape flavor. "Sweet sugars,"

she said. "The taste is there . . . but not the color."

"Winter white jelly beans." Raina grinned. "I like them!" She tossed a few into her mouth and smiled. "Well done, Berry."

The two fairy princesses arrived at the meadow. "We all need help sometimes," Princess Sprinkle said. "And I am glad that I was here to lend a hand."

"And a few barrels of cocoa," Dash added.

The two princesses laughed.

The Candy Fairies drew closer together. Seeing the sisters hug made them feel closer to one another. They had done a sweet thing. Now they could rejoice in the sweet ending to the jelly bean jumble.

FIND OUT

WHAT HAPPENS IN

The Chocolate Rose

Cocoa the Chocolate Fairy woke up early. She stretched her golden wings and looked out her window. She was eager to get outside and check on her garden.

Just a few weeks ago Cocoa had visited her older cousin Mocha, and her cousin had given her special chocolate flower seedlings to plant in her own garden. Every day for the last week, Cocoa woke up extra early to see if the buds were opening. Maybe today the seedlings would flower!

Mocha had a real gift with flowers. Her garden was known far and wide for its beauty and the vivid colors of each blossom. She lived in Sugar Kingdom and had a very important job: She was the chief gardener and tended to the Royal Palace's flowers for King Crunch and Queen Sweetie, Princess Lolli and Princess Sprinkle's parents. Cocoa was so proud of her!

When Cocoa reached her garden, she was happy to see little stems peeking through the brown-sugar soil.

"Good morning," she said to the seedlings. She bent down and watered the tiny chocolate stems with her watering can. Carefully, she sprinkled water on the center flower. This was a chocolate rose.

"You are doing just fine," she whispered to the tiny seedling. "I will take care of you. Mocha told me what to do."

Normally, chocolate roses did not bloom in Sugar Valley, but Cocoa was determined to grow one. The first thing she did when she came home from visiting Mocha was plant the seedlings. She spread chocolate sprinkles around the stems just as she had seen her do.

Cocoa sat down on a large rock candy next to the garden and admired her work. She had cleared the flower bed herself. She had turned the sugar soil and put rock candy along the edges. Cocoa dreamed of having a garden filled with flowers. The garden was not as fancy as the ones at the king and queen's palace or at Mocha's, but this garden was all hers.

"*Sweeeeeeet* morning!" a voice called from above.

Cocoa looked up and saw her Caramel Fairy friend. Melli's wings were fluttering fast. Cocoa could tell that Melli was bursting with news.

"What's the good word?" Cocoa called.

Melli came swooping down. Her excitement made her wings move quickly, and she floated above Cocoa.

"Princess Lolli's parents, King Crunch and Queen Sweetie, are coming to Candy Kingdom!" Melli exclaimed.

"The king and queen are coming *here*?" Cocoa asked. She had never met the royal couple. She knew them from their large portraits in Princess Lolli's throne room. The king and queen lived in the Royal Palace in Sugar Kingdom. They looked like sweet and kind fairies. A visit from them was a very big deal! "Princess Lolli must be so excited that her parents are coming," she added.

"She is," Melli told her. "In honor of their visit, there is going to be a royal talent show on the shore of Chocolate River." Melli did a flip in the air. "How sweet is that?"

"A talent show?" Cocoa repeated.

"Princess Lolli thought it would be a great idea," Melli replied. "I think it is a *sugar-tastic* one! Don't you?"

Cocoa's wings twitched.

"All the fairies in the kingdom are being asked

to help build the outdoor stage," Melli went on.

"An outdoor stage?" Cocoa asked.

"Yes!" Melli cried. She did a few more flips high in the air. "The show is next week." She landed next to Cocoa and sat down on the rock. "I am going to play my new licorice-stick clarinet!" she said, giggling.

Cocoa smiled at her friend. Melli was too excited to stay still. Even though she was sitting, her wings were still fluttering. Melli loved playing her licorice-stick. She had been taking lessons, and she practiced all the time. A talent show was the perfect event for her to show off her new instrument. "That is great, Melli," Cocoa said. "You are going to steal the show."

"I don't know about that," Melli said. She

leaped up and stood in front of Cocoa. She studied her friend. "What's wrong?"

"Nothing," Cocoa said quickly. "I . . . well . . . I don't—"

"What are you going to do for the show?" Melli asked, interrupting her.

Cocoa looked down at the ground. Her wings drooped. "Oh, I don't know," she said.

Melli looked at her. "How come you don't seem excited about this? All the fairies in the kingdom are buzzing about this news."

Cocoa got up and walked closer to her flowers. "I am," she said. "I am excited to see the king and the queen."

"What about the show?" Melli asked.

"I don't know," Cocoa said softly. She sat back down on the rock.

"I am sure you can do an act with Berry, Raina, or Dash," Melli said quickly. "For sure, they will all want to be a part of this. Who wouldn't want to be in the royal talent show?"

Cocoa watched Melli twirl around. She knew someone who wouldn't want to be center stage—herself! She didn't have the heart to tell Melli. Melli was usually so shy and unsure. Now look at her! She was excited about performing. Cocoa sighed. Melli had real talent and loved playing her instrument. She would be a perfect act.

"We will all be in the show together," Melli went on. "And imagine, we'll get to perform for King Crunch and Queen Sweetie! Princess Lolli will be so proud!"

Cocoa lowered her head. She didn't know how to tell her friend she was not planning on having any part in the event. Thinking about standing onstage in front of all those fairies—and the king and queen—made her heart race. If only she had a musical talent like Melli did! But Cocoa couldn't hum a tune, let alone play an instrument. There was no way she could get onstage to be in the talent show—especially in front of the king and queen!